D1217593

The Retired Kid

Jon Agee

Hyperion Books for Children

AN IMPRINT OF DISNEY BOOK GROUP

To Lucia and Emilio

It's hard work being a kid. First of all, there's school.

Then there's soccer practice,

violin class,

voice lessons,

walking Sparky,

babysitting
your little sister,

not to mention having
to eat your vegetables!

So, one day, Brian decided to retire.
"It's been a wonderful eight years," he said,
"but I need a break."

His parents thought he was joking, so they threw him a retirement party.

But Brian was serious.
The next day, he flew to Florida,
to the Happy Sunset Retirement Community.

T COMMUNITY

Happy Sunset was a lovely place.
There was a swimming pool,
tennis courts, and a snack bar.
"Wow!" thought Brian,
"I should have retired years ago."

Happy Sunset was full of interesting people.
There was Ethel, Wally, Tex, Myrtle, and Phyllis.

And there was Harvey, a retired plumber.
"So, what did you used to do?" he asked Brian.
"Uh, I was a kid."
"A kid?" said Harvey. "That's hard work!"

Being retired was *not* hard work.
There were card games.

There was golf.

There were long afternoon naps.

Some days, Harvey took Brian fishing,

to a ball game,

or to the movies.
"So, what do you think, kid?" he said.
"Isn't retirement a blast?"

But Brian wasn't sure. Being retired meant having to listen to Tex go on and on about his hip replacement,

looking at hundreds of snapshots of Myrtle's grandchildren,

or watching long documentaries on TV.

There were other things, too,
like early morning yoga,

knitting classes,

weekly checkups
(when Brian wasn't
even feeling sick!),

Friday-night swing dancing,

Wally's prune juice smoothies,

not to mention sitting
on Ethel's false teeth!

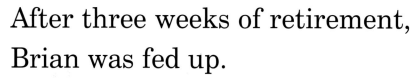

After three weeks of retirement,
Brian was fed up.
"It's no use," he said. "I don't fit in."

"Listen, kid," said Harvey,
"when retirement gets you down,
   you have to think back
   to the good old days."
"The good old days?"
"Never fails,"
   said Harvey.

So, Brian found a quiet spot under a palm tree and thought back to the good old days.

Very soon he started remembering things. Good things—like the time he scored a goal for the soccer team,

the time he aced his math test,

the time he hit the
perfect note on his violin!

He remembered singing
in the school musical,

making his
little sister laugh,

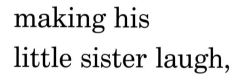

throwing Sparky the ball!

He even remembered that broccoli wasn't so bad if you covered it with cheddar cheese.

Brian made up his mind.
"Hey, Harvey," he said,
"I've decided to come out of retirement."
Harvey wasn't surprised.
"Well, I'll miss you, kid."

The next morning, Brian packed his things
and wished everybody at Happy Sunset the best.
Then he caught the first flight back home.

His parents were happy to see him.

So were his teachers and all of his pals.
"It's hard work being a kid," said Brian,
"but guess what?"